The Story of a Boy and Autism Unawareness

(A "Bea" Story)

Beatriz Fox

Meant 2 Bea Publications
Newport Beach, CA

Note to Reader: This is the story of a boy who is unable to adequately voice his feelings (from actual events) told from the point of view of his mother. It is the brainchild of a blog that can be found at:

http://chriswillblog.wordpress.com/

Meant 2 Bea Publications
Newport Beach, CA

Paperback Edition: April 2013

LCCN: 2013900135

ISBN-10 0615728235

ISBN-13 - 978-0-615-72823-0

10 9 8 7 6 5 4 3 2

Book Design by Mike Hernandez

Photography by Matt Ramirez & Beatriz Fox

Printed in the United States of America

I dedicate this story and all the days of my life to the loves of my life: Christopher, Mila, and Dots (Woof, woof!)

The Autism Diagnosis was about:

1 in 5000 in the 1970s
1 in 2500 in the 1980s
1 in 500 in the 1990s
1 in 250 in 2001
1 in 166 in 2004
1 in 150 in 2007
1 in 110 in 2009
1 in 88 in 2012

Today in 2013, it is estimated that one (1) in every 50 school-aged children in the United States have some form of autism.

Table of Contents

Chris Seemed to Have it All

Autism is a complex disorder that affects brain development. The aftermath can include deficits in social skills, communication, repetitive behaviors and/or interests, or all of the above. A person with autism may have co-morbid conditions such as gross or fine motor issues, attention deficits, gastrointestinal issues, sleep disturbances, obsessive compulsive disorder, epilepsy, sensory integration disorder, Tourette's Syndrome, etcetera. My son, Chris seemed to have it all.

Prologue

"White Picket Fence" Theory

My name is Beatriz (bee-uh-TREEZ...) "Bea," for short. I grew up in Alhambra, California and was raised in a middle class family. I was determined to be more than a statistic. My status quo constantly changed, as I juggled work, school, and attempted to have some semblance of a social life. I was 18.

In college, one of my favorite "poster-sayings" was of a photograph of a breathtaking mansion with multiple sports cars parked in front of this magnificent dream home. The caption read, "Justification for Higher Education." I often thought of the words and images on that motivational poster, and it inspired me to work towards my dreams with education being at the forefront of my pursuit. I was fixated on the man whom I felt would catapult "our" dream into fruition. I assumed he would come first (on his white horse and in his modern day knight's clothing, of course. We would live "happily ever after with our 2.5 kids." That was my "white picket fence" theory.

"Plan Bea"

At age 28 my plan had still not come to be and my patience had worn. I felt the need to reassess my foolproof plan and come up with another. For the first time in my life, I took the baby and man out of my fairy tale equation and was left with the most important players in my life: Bea, myself and I. I felt born again, if only for a moment. I believed that if my "white picket fence" theory were to come true, I had to be my own "Knight in Shining Armor" and save myself.

My new plan would be to focus on me. I was committed to marrying my career and forsaking all others in the process. I had a renewed spirit and take on life and all of its endless possibilities. I was anxious to finish school, travel, and (you know) rule the world. My possibilities were endless. And in that moment as I "took breath" into my body, I was filled with the energizing beauty of hope. I was focused on reinventing my new beginning on "The Road Less Traveled." My new plan would be called "Plan Bea."

BEATRIZ FOX

What is Meant to "Bea will "Bea"

I felt excited and empowered with my new Plan Bea in motion. I worked at the LA Times and reaped the rewards of being one of the top salespersons in advertising. I also attended Film School at Loyola Marymount University (a premier Catholic University in Westchester) where I lived on campus. Less than a month into my new "Plan Bea," I found out that I was pregnant. I guess that's the irony of life. I've always believed everything happens for a reason and what is "meant to 'Bea' will 'Bea.'"

Baby-to-"Bea"

The school semester was over mid-December 1999. I moved from campus to Alhambra before settling in to Burbank. My last day of work was Friday, January 21. I ended up in the hospital late that very night, because my water broke. I wanted to give birth naturally, and held out as long as the doctors said it was safe to do so. However, after an 18+-hour labor, I ended up having a C-section (because I never dilated past four.) Soon, there would be a "baby to Bea."

"It's a Boy!"

On the day my son joined Planet Earth, the world of "Bea, myself and I" would no longer "Bea;" since I had a "bran' spankin' new "mini Bea!" He was a beautiful 7lb, 1oz. bouncing baby "He." MY son? Wow. It was real. He was real. This was real. It was January 23rd, 2000; And, I had a son that I named Christopher William... Now what? I wasn't sure; but I was so excited for our future. After all of these months I could finally say, "It's a boy!

Life was Good

After Chris's birth, I worked around-the-clock (from home) but he was within eyesight and/or earshot 24/7. I based my breaks around his waking hours so we could have mommy-son time and bond like super glue. I hooked him up with a crib that had enough stimulating colors, toys, and attachments that would make a blind man swear he could see. I bought every type of baby learning video that existed and had them constantly playing on our television.

My days were long and grueling: alternating between work, diaper changes, and play. However, I had never been more disciplined or determined to succeed in my life. Chris happily adjusted to his baby duties: Eating, sleeping, and producing the inevitable loads of diapers! Life was good.

Intuitive Whisper

After Christopher's birth I went to a Pediatrician who followed a non-traditional immunization schedule. I wasn't sure if I should be excited or concerned. The world of mom was new to me, and my choices of pediatricians were extremely limited with my cobra health insurance and no other option. My rationale: There was an office full of children, so what could go wrong? This is what I said out loud, but in my mind doubt was cast by an intuitive whisper.

Mindblind - 2003

The future: December 2003. Christopher was three-years old. (He lost his spontaneous speech at age one, after an MMR shot.) One doctor told me that he would never speak. I begged to differ, because he did have one consistent word for me when I gave him a demand..."No!" He didn't like the feel of water. If immersed in a bath, he would scream bloody murder. The flushing sound of a toilet caused him to cover his ears in pain, and flicking the light switch off and on was an obsessive pleasure. (But wasn't it for other children?)

Chris had a high tolerance for pain. When he became frustrated he would use his hands and feet to convey his upset to me, because his words were lost. It was like going to battle with my body being the target of his blows and kicks. He didn't like to be held and showed no emotional regard for anyone other than himself. A Psychiatrist told me to institutionalize him because he was mindblind.

Mindblind - Poem

The inability of a person to empathize
The inability of a person to surmise
The inability to understand how others feel
This condition with Autism is real
Emotions, they may not recognize
No sparkling twinkle in their eye
It may seem as though they do not care
Their expression may resemble a blank stare
"Mindblind," in order to abate...
Treatment is necessary. Do not wait
Prevent alienation. Promote ABA/inclusion
So the ASD population can join as one

Once Upon A Time

Once upon a time there lived a "typical" atypical boy. Though there are other players of interest in this story; this is, in its simplest form, "The Story of a Boy" (and autism unawareness.)

The Beginning – January 23, 2000

January 23rd became the best day of my life thus far, because on that day I became a mother to a beautiful baby boy who I named Christopher. His middle name, William, was chosen in honor of my father and symbolic of my belief that Chris "will" (do/be/have anything/everything in life!) Words like "can't" or "won't" wouldn't exist in our household... My mantra was simple: "Chris will."

Valentine's Day - 2000

Dear Christopher,
You are I, and I am you... We are one! You are my dream come true, and I love you with all of my heart. Happy 1st Valentine's Day!

Love, Mommy!

Valentine's Day - 2000
- From actual card

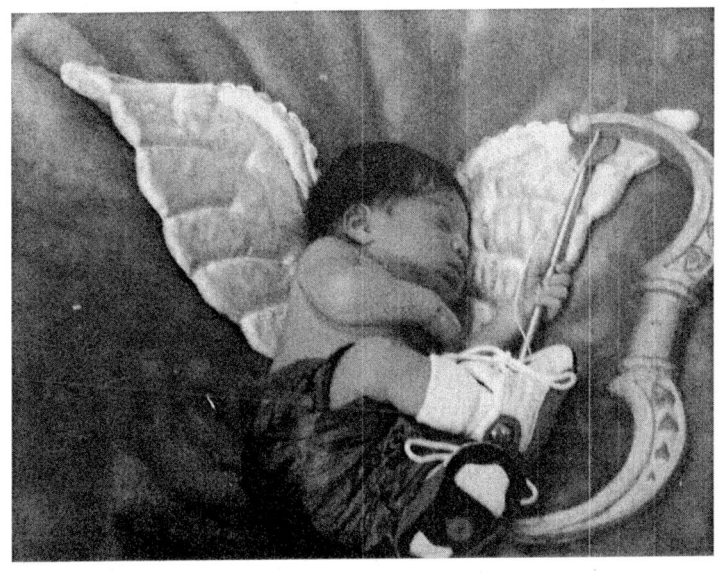

No Worries

What change a year can bring! I took things in stride year one, acclimating to my new life as Christopher's mommy; and, prepared for baby number two. I adored Christopher, and it was no secret that he was my "everything." Christopher got all of me, that first year. I spoiled him shamelessly...

Nothing but the best for baby Chris! I shopped for his baby stroller with the same vigor as I imagined I would when buying his first car. The winner: A Peg Perego Sherpa style stroller imported from Italy. I pushed him around the streets of Burbank (be it day or night) for his pleasure and my exercise.

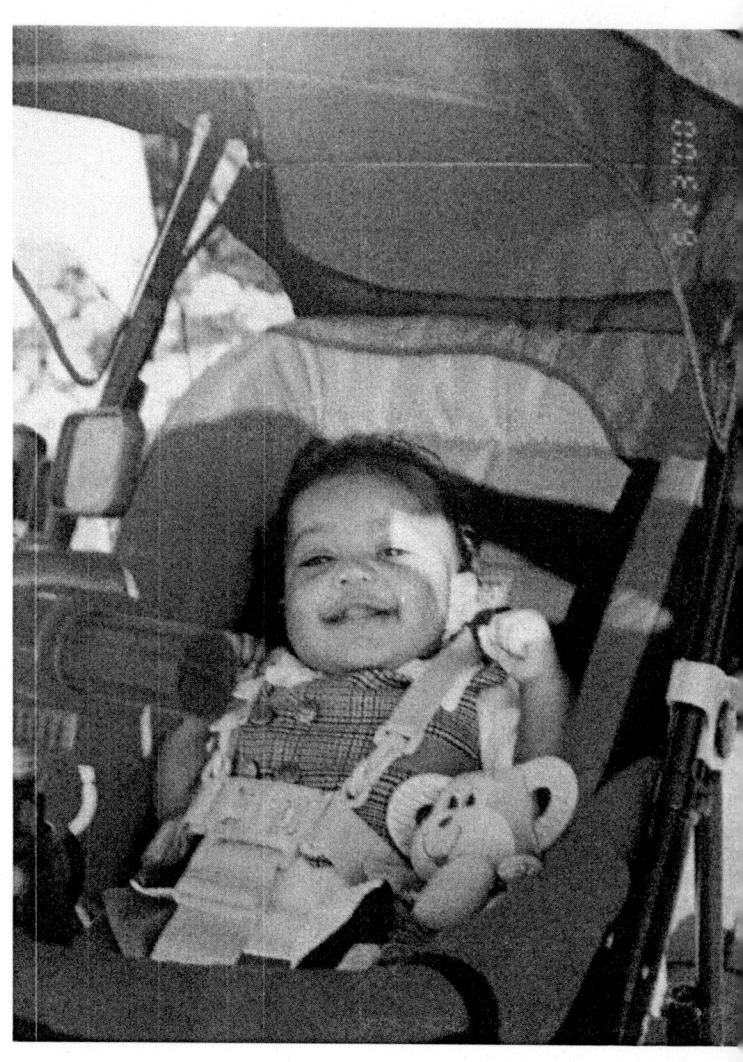

My obsession was taking daily pictures of Christopher to capture every moment of his life on film. Everything he did was joyful and wondrous to me. Chris was smiling, rolling over, grabbing, playing peek-a-boo, and sitting up [by four (4) months...] There were no worries.

Lights, Camera, Action!

I was like the "Energizer Bunny," and in love with the possibilities of life. I held steadfast to the idea that with hard work and determination our dreams could come true. I submitted Christopher's photo to a talent agency. He was readily signed and started working in the entertainment industry. Lights. Camera. Action!

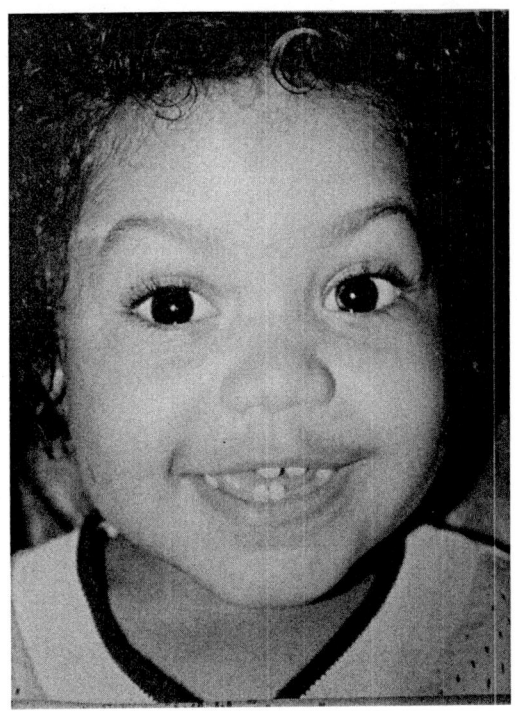

"In Sickness and in Health"

At seven months, I brought Christopher in for an immunization because it was scheduled. However, I let the doctor immediately know that he was sick. I wanted Chris to be seen, but I didn't want him to get a shot. "I had heard," I explained, "that a baby wasn't supposed to be given a vaccine shot when he was sick." The nurse took him from me to do vitals in another room, as I voiced my concerns to the doctor. The doctor left the room. When she came back, I was notified that Chris was given the immunizations without my consent.

I was livid. The doctor was emotionless. She looked me straight in the eye and said that he would be fine. I trusted doctors then (I was naïve.) I didn't know then what an uphill battle Chris and I would soon have, but no matter what the struggle, I vowed to be by his side (in sickness and in health.)

The Aftermath of "That Shot"

After receiving "that shot," Christopher's condition rapidly declined with each new day. It took nearly two weeks before his pediatrician took my pleas for help seriously (though I called, went into the office or both almost daily.) I would report to the pediatrician that Chris was losing weight, for instance, [at seven months old] and her response would be, "You're small. Maybe the baby is thinning out." My face was stoic at the absurdity of her suggestion that a baby could "thin out" at seven months.

My mind ran rampant, desperate to get through to this doctor so that I could help my son. But it took nearly two weeks before she realized the extent of her neglect. At the moment of her awakening, she became fearful and panicked. She wanted to call 911 on the spot so he could be rushed to the hospital. I refused, taking him in myself so that I could stay by his side and comfort him. He was readily admitted.

Unfortunately, I learned the hard way that it is sometimes necessary to be wary of doctors. A mommy's intuition towards her child trumps a doctorate degree on many a day. When Christopher's doctor looked at him, she did not "see" him. She discounted the dark circles and extremely darkened "bags" (under his eyes) that marked him like eye black. She was unconcerned with his weight loss. She discounted all of his early warning signs. I was ignored and given nonsensical explanations as to what was happening to Chris.

I was left feeling helpless and hapless, as I watched Christopher deteriorate and wither away right before my erratic, weepy eyes. My baby was gravely ill but no one saw it but me. Because it happened so fast, I was unable to switch to another doctor. The lack of quality care provided to Christopher by this pediatric office was sub-standard and deplorable. The hospital had to be better (I prayed) for Christopher's sake. It was surreal that my baby was clinging to life because of an immunization shot. But it was his reality and the aftermath of "that shot."

Proceed with Caution

Chris was in the hospital an entire week and there was no treatment plan in place. His diagnosis: "failure to thrive." I was not producing enough milk to adequately breastfeed. My Obstetrician told me that if I increased my food intake, my breast milk would come back. His "theory" was false.

Christopher's pediatrician gave me a prescription that she swore would increase my breast milk. When I went to fill it, the Pharmacist told me that the medication would be harmful to my unborn baby. I questioned the pediatrician, asking her why she would prescribe a medication that was dangerous to my unborn child. Her answer: "I forgot." I put so much faith into the "assumed" wisdom of doctors, (sometimes) undeservedly so. What I was learning (too little, too late) was that "doctor" was a title, and it was in my best interest to proceed with caution!

Going Under the Knife

Hospital Stay/Week Two – The doctors wanted to cut Christopher's stomach open to put a feeding tube in. I was mortified and had never been more frantic in my life. I pleaded with them to try anything else. How invasive and unnecessary! Why couldn't something/anything less intrusive be tried first?

Long breath in, slow breath out, followed by a panicked sigh... "No way!" was my answer. I would flat out refuse. It was as simple as that. I could get Christopher to take the milk another way. I was sure of it. I was his mother. I would find a way, because that's what mothers do. Now, if I failed, of course I would be open to exploring other options. But, in my eyes it was not an acceptable or logical "Plan A" to senselessly subject a baby to "going under the knife."

"Eyes Wide Shut"

Why was it suddenly urgent to cut Christopher's stomach open and put a feeding tube with such haste? I had been by Christopher's bedside for an entire week; and there was no talk of any kind of "game plan" for increasing his milk intake. Why was surgery Plan A? Was this money-driven? Was it just a quicker/easier route to take? Or both? I didn't know; and I didn't care. I would fight this decision with the hope of protecting Christopher (who had no voice in the matter.)

The doctor-in-charge at the hospital (from Christopher's pediatric office) was pompous, at best. He walked around exuding a stench of one who felt superior to everyone, because of his "title." Everything else was unsubstantial to him. He was the doctor and what he said would be with no regard to who he hurt. That was my take on him, anyway.

This was unacceptable to me. He was unacceptable to me. When it came to my son, I had the strength within to fight a dozen grown men, aliens from another planet, in/at Armageddon... no matter. I was fearless. In knowing that I was unwavering in my refusal to allow the doctors to cut open Christopher's stomach to insert a feeding tube (as a first option) so the head doctor brought Social Services into this matter. (Social Services, really!!) An emergency meeting was called with countless doctors, hospital staff, Social Services, and little ol' me. I felt as if I were a misguided Girl Scout Leader trapped in a boxing match fighting for my son's life against a pack of wolves in scrub suits. DING. End of round one with me (a.k.a. "the Underdog") cornered with my "Eyes Wide Shut."

52

For Chris, I Will

I stepped into the role of advocate for Chris and fought for "Plan Bea: An Alternative to Surgery." I presented my case with reason, passion and intellect, minus the doctor "lingo." In the midst of this battle, I found out that surgery was not normally the hospital's "Plan A." There was another option. (My heart skipped a beat; then raced seemingly faster than a driver in the Indy 500.) It was called a Supplemental Nursing System "SNS."

The SNS was simply a feeding tube that a nursing mother could attach to her breast. The tube was connected to a bottle that was filled with formula. If the baby was successful with sucking the tube he should be able to adequately sustain his milk intake needs. In the end, I was given 24 hours (no exceptions) to successfully have Christopher drink milk from the SNS. If I failed, they would do the operation without my consent. I closed my eyes knowing the odds were not in our favor and thought: for Chris, I will!.

Exit Stage Left

Let me just cut to the chase... we did it!
And, in LESS than the 24 hours allotted.
Christopher did it! I just knew (prayed) he
would. The odds were stacked against us,
but in the end, we prevailed. Together, we'd
rule the world... one day!

When Christopher's doctors and the social
worker arrived, their smiles faded as they
focused on "the Pink Elephant in the room"
(i.e. Christopher, who contentedly drank milk
from his supplemental nursing system.) It
was at that moment that I mentally affirmed
that these doctors were most definitely not
rooting for or on "Team Christopher."

Their eyes: In a uniformed/ uncontrolled
state of disbelief. Neither the doctors nor
the social worker verbally acknowledged our
accomplishment. "Plan Bea" had not only
prevailed, but at a rate that all of them
believed was impossible. They overlooked
the power of true love. No matter. The
drama was over, and it was time for Team
Christopher to exit stage left!

Halloween - 2000

To my little pumpkin, Christopher,
(It's your first Halloween!) I love you with all
of my heart! You and I have been sick for a
week so we didn't get around to Trick-or-
Treating. Instead, we are handing out candy.
So far, only two kids have come to our
door. Trick-or-Treating has really changed!
(Sad face)

Love, Mommy!
* From actual card

CHRIStmas - 2000

To the love in/of my life, Christopher I love you more than words could ever express. I hope you think you've got a great mommy, because I know I have a great son! (Happy face.) Times are kind of tough for me this Christmas, but I will do my best to make sure you experience the love, beauty and simple joys of Christmas day. I love you with all of my heart.

Love, Mommy! ~ CHRIStmas – 2000
  • From actual card

New Year's – 2001

Dear Christopher,
This first year of your life has been wonderful yet challenging. We have spent an entire year together getting to know each other. Next year (or this new year!) you will have to get used to having a brother or sister to share the limelight that has been yours alone this past year. Your brother or sister is due on your birthday. Hopefully you will enjoy that, as you get older! You have all of my love, forever. (Happy face)

Love, Mommy!
 • From actual card

We spent the evening watching and waiting for the ball to drop on New Year's Rockin' Eve. I've heard it said that what you do on New Year's is indicative of how you'll spend the coming year. I spent the evening with your sister snug inside of me, and you by my side. And being with the two of you was happiness at its best. There was no other place on earth that I'd have rather been but with the two of you.

Ain't Love Grand

On January 17, 2001, Mila Grace was born. Christopher had a baby sister. She was beautiful and perfect. It was surreal that I had a boy and a girl, just like I'd always dreamed of. I now had two loves of my life. Ain't love grand!

The MMR

At 12 months, Christopher had his first words: "dada and juice." They were not necessarily in that order, but they were right on schedule. Then came the MMR vaccine right after his first birthday, and the spontaneous speech tapered off like a person standing by your side who quietly "tip-toed" away without your knowledge, leaving you dazed and confused.

Christopher had spontaneous speech, but then it left. Where, when and why it went was then unknown? I now believe it was the MMR.

- Thimerosal is a compound that was first introduced by Eli Lilly and Company in 1929. It was used as a preservative in some vaccines. The use of thimerosal can cause mercury poisoning, which is believed (by some) to be one cause for certain types of autism.

Mercury-Tainted Shots?

There are no less than two times that I suspect that Chris had definite life-altering reactions to an immunization shot. The first was at seven months (the shot was an IPV.) The second was at one year (that shot was the MMR.)

I strongly believe that Christopher should not have been given an immunization shot when he was sick at seven months. I also believe that the immunization shots that he received were tainted with Thimerosal (a mercury-containing compound/preservative used in some vaccines for children.)

Is mercury simply a nice way of saying poison? Mercury is a poisonous metallic element. And contrary to what many believe, thimerosal is still used today in vaccines, in varying degrees. This being the case, would it be safe to conclude that some vaccines are in essence mercury-tainted shots?

"Something Just Ain't Right"

The coming year was hectic: Juggling work, alternating between breastfeeding, diaper changes; and dividing my attention between Mila and Chris. Mila started meeting her milestones, while Christopher's became stagnant. Year two of motherhood is when I started presenting my observations and fears to the doctors that I took him to, but they were blind to his delays.

Christopher lost his spontaneous speech almost as quickly as he got it. There was a period when Chris didn't speak at all; then when he spoke again, his speech was rote. His pediatrician's explanation was: "Girls develop faster than boys." (Here we go again!)

I didn't have other children around Christopher and Mila or I surely would have pushed the issue of "what" could be wrong with Christopher differently. Rather, Christopher's well-baby doctor visits were all coming back with stars. Still, I had an underlying timidity from within. Every time I tried to voice my concerns to Christopher's doctor, he shushed my fears away and told me everything was fine. So I left his office doubting myself, having felt like I was one of "those" mothers who panicked needlessly and/or seemed to over-exaggerate situations. I put my fears on the "back burner" and carried around my imaginary "Linus Blanket," hoping all was right in our world.

If ALL of the doctors were saying Christopher was all right, I must be wrong to keep pushing the issue, right? I was not assured. I felt like a magnet for the flock of inefficient, disconnected doctors in the world. I didn't know what was wrong with Christopher, but my mother's intuition said, "Something just ain't right."

By Default

We stayed in Burbank until Mila was nearly a year old, but life was stagnant. I felt a change would be good for us. So, I packed my car; and Christopher, Mila and I drove off towards our new life, not for certain where that may "Bea."

My heart was leading me towards San Francisco; but, on a whim, I headed up north in the heart of what I realized was rush hour traffic. Three hours later, we had only made it as far as Santa Barbara. Exhaustion set in and made me re-think my plan. I loved Santa Barbara and the beach; so, why not make some roots? San Francisco was a bust, so Santa Barbara became our new "home-sweet-home" by default.

This Time...

Santa Barbara was the most laid back place we ever lived. I laughed when my neighbor told me we lived in the ghetto. "Santa Barbara has a ghetto?" I asked. But come mid-morning when the train passed our apartments, I knew what she meant. Our place shook so violently that it felt like we were in a major earthquake... daily.

Shortly after moving, I enrolled Chris and Mila in daycare. It was at that time, when I saw Christopher interact with other children his age, that the thought resurfaced that something was wrong. Then one day I unexpectedly received a call from the daycare alarming me of a happenstance...

"Chris was fine," they told me. But there was a big piece of equipment that came crashing down right behind him. "He wasn't hit," I was assured. But they were concerned, because he didn't even flinch. A possible hearing impairment... I might finally have an answer as to what was wrong with Christopher, this time...

Another Closed Door

I voiced my concerns to the new pediatrician about Christopher. He examined him then accusingly asked, "Do you talk to him?" Did I hear him correctly? Seriously!! He was my first-born. I talked to him so much it was a wonder that his little ears didn't fall off! And Mila was right there yakking like her life depended on it. Did he think she and I went off on talk sessions while I locked him in a closet?

My face drew a blank, and I was very cautious with my answer, because sarcasm tends to roll from my mouth like a red carpet at a Hollywood movie premiere, when provoked. "Of course." I firmly replied. But the doctor shook his head, disbelieving and went on to ask, "If you talk to him, why isn't he talking?"

I needed a doctor's help, not a misguided interrogation. The doctor referred me to an audiologist, as I requested. The audiologist said Christopher's hearing was perfect. No additional referral was made, leaving us with yet another closed door.

Professional Beach Bums

When I say Christopher wasn't talking, I mean that he stopped having spontaneous speech. Oddly, he could repeat the entire alphabet through "tell me what you think of me," after watching his favorite Sesame Street Video. He found comfort in putting pieces of clothing over his head. And, in lieu of toys, he was fixated on objects. He had no safety awareness.

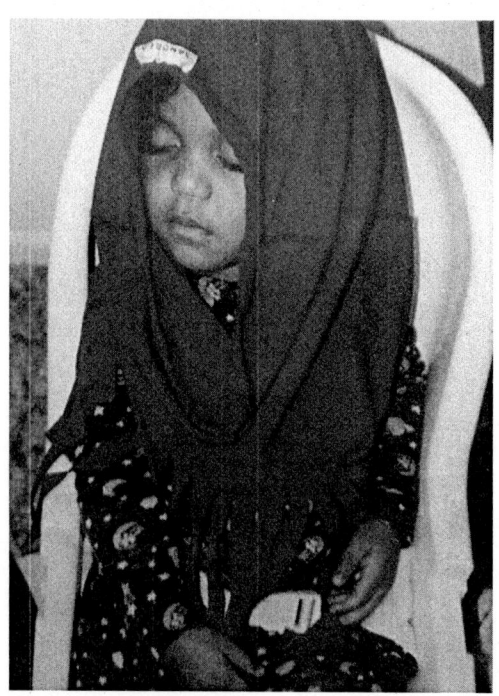

I loved the Santa Barbara area and vibe. Everybody knew everybody, and the atmosphere was so relaxed. No honking horns or excess noise. But there was also no hope of a good job for someone without a degree. It was a great life in a different circumstance. I had no silver spoon in my mouth so it wasn't a stretch to determine that if I stayed, we were going to be subjected to a lifetime of poverty, and our future may be limited to becoming being professional beach bums.

"... She was Wrong."

New home: Old Town, Pasadena. I re-enrolled at LMU, and started Christopher and Mila in my university's daycare. Christopher was hyperactive, and interested in exploring everything... or, at least, specific things. Everyone quickly found that his interest was in locks. He spied the keys and unlocked the gates so all of the children could run free. My son, a freedom fighter!

The staff was frustrated, at times. It could be difficult to deal with Christopher's intense, scattered energy. Then, one day a classroom aide hesitantly approached me. She told me she thought Christopher had autism. Autism? (No. What's that? No... No?)

I had no visual reference of autism other than a movie I had seen with Dustin Hoffman and Tom Cruise called, "Rain Man." She went on to tell me I should contact a regional center so he could be assessed. I certainly didn't believe her or want to believe her; however, I scheduled an appointment so I could check it off my list when they told me she was wrong.

MY Son Has Autism?

I took Christopher for an assessment at a Regional Center, because I wanted to leave no stone unturned; however, in no way did I feel that Christopher had autism. After testing him, which consisted of talking to/playing with him, the psychologist felt that he met the diagnostic criteria for autistic disorder, based on the DSM-IV-TR. She broke the news to me as gently as someone who "breaks the news" to people for her everyday job could. My first question was, "Can you do more testing to make sure?" But she said it wasn't necessary. I politely nodded, though not in agreement. I felt like she was speaking a language foreign to me. I could hear her words, but my mind refused to process them.

The psychologist was going to refer Christopher to his school district for a special education evaluation to begin the process for an Individual Education Plan (IEP) to address educational and academic needs. In addition, she recommended that he begin an intensive in-home applied behavioral analysis program (ABA) to address maladaptive behaviors, increase self-help skills, and social skills. Next she recommended parent education, training, therapy, classes and support. She made further recommendations for a Speech and Occupational Therapy evaluation to determine his adaptive motor delays and sensory integration deficits.

This would be after I had an Individualized Program Plan (IPP) meeting at Regional Center with Christopher's Service Coordinator (once assigned.) Lastly, she wanted the names and numbers of all of the doctors that I had gone to since Christopher was a baby so that she could send them information on autism awareness. She was appalled that all of his previous doctors missed his early warning signs indicative of autism. There was that word again... the "A" word. Wait. Did she just say MY son has autism?

Breathe

I had no idea what the Psychologist said. My brain shut down after hearing, "Your son has autism." I felt like I had been catapulted into a retro-Charlie Brown TV Special where I was a student in his class. All I heard was: "Wah wah wah wah wah." I broke into a sweat and the room started to spin like an out-of-control carousel. Autism. How could my son have that?

I zoned out so I wouldn't break into a "Niagara Falls" cry or pass out. I glanced at my children, with my eyes lingering a little longer than usual on Christopher. Tears welled my eyes like a clogged drain. Then I returned my focus back to the psychologist. My nod was precise and on cue... as though manipulated by the World's best puppeteer.

I was on "information overload" and had to escape. I forced a smile and motioned towards the door. I gathered Christopher, Mila, my purse, the diaper bag, stroller, books, and hightailed it out of there. I began to run, but felt as though I was running in quicksand and couldn't breathe.

Breathe - Poem

My head: In the clouds, everything seemingly
right... Then I took a wrong turn
Stepped onto sand, and quick as a light,
sank into a dreadful fright
Initially grounded, but then I fell far below
Devoid of sunrays, in the land of dismay
Help me, dear God, so I may win this fight
For my two young kids, show me the light
The sand covered me straight to my head
And this is what my inner voice said:
"I help those in life who help themselves"
Then intellectually I was able to delve
No longer trapped from within
Had a second chance to start life again
Probably be different than previously thought
Nonetheless, 'twas the miracle I sought
When life throws you into a metaphoric
quicksand, look no further than the invisible
hand (from above)
And, breathe...

True Love

I had no idea what autism was, and that left me feeling off-kilter. It was a spectrum disorder, I learned, that ranged from low functioning/mentally challenged to savant. That, to me, was not a range... it was a polar opposite. So where did that leave Christopher?

I was told that Christopher's autism seemed moderate, but that could change for the better or worse as he got older. His skill levels were uneven and scattered, which made it difficult to assess and say for sure. (In other words, they didn't know.

I was told that there was no cure for autism. (No cure... Was it a disease?) But yet I had all of these books by parent authors that said they cured their child of autism. (At least, those were the ones I chose to read.) Show me the cure! I would do whatever I needed to do so that Chris could/would recover. My sacrifice for he and Mila would know no bounds ever. Because, to me, that is true love...

True Love - Poem

For the love of your child, what all would
you do
Would you give up the dreams that you
used to pursue
What if your child was not mentally well
And, deep into solitude, he progressively fell
Would you redefine yourself and start life
anew
For the love of your child, what all would
you do
If you thought it was possible to nurse him
back to health
Would you give up all that's considered
material wealth
In the face of sadness or unspeakable pain
When you have everything to lose; and,
maybe, nothing is gained
Would you be strong or walk away
Would you stand tall or crumble with dismay
What all would you do, for the love of your
child
As for me, I'd do anything just to see mine
smile
For the love of my child, I simply do
For the love of my child is true love

Journey to Autism and Back

After playing the "blame game" with myself, I had a multitude of emotions that surfaced. Amongst them was fear. Christopher was my first-born, and I was still learning how to be the mom of a "typical" child. I didn't know how to raise a child with autism. How would I do it? What was autism anyway? Thank goodness for "Google" and libraries...

It helped reading about the journey of other parents of children with autism, because it served as a roadmap to where I may be headed with Christopher. I encountered doctors that said my son would never talk or who told me to put Chris in an institution because it would be difficult for me to raise him. I shunned those types of "doctors." I would cure Christopher of autism, (if that was possible) no matter how many years it took on this journey to Autism and back.

The Storm Before the Rainbow

Lots of questions about Christopher were answered with each new book I read on autism. Come to find, autism was a world in and of itself that I knew nothing about. In my mind, I was adamant that Chris did not do the things associated with autism; then I would turn around and gasp as I began to see everything I read come to life right before my tearful eyes.

In spite of the challenges, Christopher was a joy. In general, he was a happy boy. Through therapy, he began to show positive change. (Baby steps, if you will.) But it was with a LOT of work. Therapy was from sunrise to bedtime every single day. The therapists transformed my house into a makeshift clinic where we would produce words, compliance, and social skills. I learned to withhold any item of interest (including food or drink) until he earned it by at least attempting to say the word. Through Applied Behavioral Analysis, he was eventually potty-trained, and he learned lots of vocabulary. It was the beginning of our journey through autism... the storm before the rainbow.

The Good, the Bad, and the Ugly

The Good: Chris loves life and is a "people" person. He loves music. His favorite radio station is KDAY-93.5, and he claps with excitement when his favorite songs play. He is curious, loves all animals, the iPad, the Vans store, paddleballs, and Tyler Perry movies. He wants nothing more than to have a friend to play/have fun with. He has a penchant for girls with brightly colored hair (especially rainbow,) and has a celebrity crush on Nicki Minaj.

The Bad: Christopher doesn't know "how" to play. He has no friends and usually plays alone. He hasn't learned the appropriate social skills to approach people or animals, and he is not safety aware. When he approaches other children, they are either afraid, indifferent or label him as strange.

The Ugly: Chris has "meltdowns" which can lead to total disorganization within his body. Due to his inability to voice his feelings, he may scream, hit and/or kick. These are some of the good, the bad, and the ugly.

A "Neurotypical" & "Atypical" Child

Autism is a world in and of itself. Today, one in 50 children in the United States are diagnosed with autism. It is the fastest growing developmental disability in the United States. If a cure is not found for this disorder, one day the child who displays "atypical" behaviors (including: rigidity, ritualism, speech difficulties and withdrawing/isolating himself from society) may be considered the new "norm/typical" child. Then society may have to redefine what it considers a "neurotypical" and/or an "atypical" child.

- Ironically, Eli Lilly and Company, (who has been accused of knowingly making, and distributing products containing thimerosal; thus, indirectly poisoning babies and children = causing the symptoms of autism) now profits from the sales of Straterra, an "Eli Lilly" drug for the treatment of Attention Deficit Hyperactivity Disorder (ADHD).
- ADHD-like symptoms are seen to be a part of the Autism Spectrum Disorder (ASD) diagnosis.

A "NeuroTypical" & "Atypical" Child - Poem

A "Neurotypical" and "Atypical child"
What exactly does that mean
Conforming to a type that society can deem
A representative specimen in which one can
relate
A distinctive characteristic that few will
negate
This defines "typical," the way that it's seen
Reminds me of the story, "Of Mice and
Men"
Where one person's strong - the other is
weak
The future of the latter is seemingly bleak
Autistic persons are labeled "Atypical," to
most
They are viewed as inferior, from coast-to-
coast
Autism: Diagnosed at 1 in 10,000 in the late
1980s
What happened that affected so many
babies
'cause in the '90s, the stats dropped to 1 in
166
One theory: Vaccines containing thimerosal
were making them sick

It's an incredulous story not meant to
mislead
About a drug company, thimerosal and
unadulterated greed
Eli Lilly and Co., named in multiple Autism
suits
The courts ruled in their favor; so is the
point now moot
What happens if the numbers continue to
fall
Will the "typical" child exist at all
Will "typical" and "atypical" be one in the
same; because the government and
pharmaceutical companies will accept no
blame

Autism Cover-Up - Poem

With the birth of my child, I felt total peace
and joy, when I heard those three life-
changing words, "IT'S – A – BOY!"
His milestones, until "that shot," he met
No way to anticipate how tough life'd get
Never imagined life could change with a
routine vaccine shot
Some say there was an Autism Cover-up
while others say, "not"
I can't speak for anyone else but me and
after my son's immunizations what I did see
An instant shot reaction that was so bad
It took away the future I dreamt he'd have
His smile turned to a frown, our lives turned
upside-down
Doctor-to-doctor, each week I went
Concerns of regression; I was eager to vent
Each new doctor had nothing new to say
Yet my son's regression was evident more
each day
He lost interest in the world, and would do
nothing but stare
I could see that my son wasn't fully aware
A daycare Aide was the only one who knew
Gave me the number to a Regional Center...
Said they would know what to do

I looked in her eyes, she was afraid to say
The diagnosis that was coming my way
I asked, "What do you think my son has?"
"Autism," she said, while looking so sad
One in 166, at the time, (diagnosed with
Autism) were the stats
How is it that MY son could have that
Mercury Toxicity, thimerosal and a vaccine
shot
I believe there was an Autism cover-up
Some believe "not"

Therapies,

2/2003 – At three years old, Christopher was responding equivalent to a 14-month old. His academic expectations would be reduced to his developmental age to promote success. His verbal/non-verbal comprehension and expressive language skills were inconsistent and equivalent to a one-year-old.

I met with a Service Coordinator (SC) at a Regional Center to work on an Individual Program Plan to discuss future objectives for Chris, and to find support and service agencies within our community.

Christopher was eligible for special education services, under the diagnosis of Autism. His deficits were in the areas of social interaction and communication. He exhibited sensory seeking and avoidance behaviors that were believed would likely significantly impact his safety at school, classroom behavior, and ability to fully access his preschool curriculum.

3/2003 – Christopher began attending a non-public school (NPS.) His initial IEP showed impairments in social interaction, communication and repetitive behaviors that would impact his educational performance. He was functioning below age level in all areas and required consistent intervention and special education support to fully access his preschool curriculum and meet his goals/objectives. (He continues to struggle with these impairments today.)

5/2003 – Christopher began Sign Language and the Picture Exchange Communication System (PECS.) Though he lacks the ability to physically "sign," due to fine motor delays, he responds more reliably with visual support. (He is currently in a Sign group at school.)

6/2003 – Christopher began receiving Occupational Therapy (OT) in a clinic setting with a Sensory Integration emphasis, and at school to assist with his classroom goals. His goals addressed: fine motor/gross motor skill development and planning, visual motor integration, sensory processing and modulation. (He continues to receive OT at school.)

7/2003- I received an invaluable report from the treatment team and Director of UCLA's

Autism Evaluation Clinic. Their recommendations/report was used as a framework for services that I would attempt to secure in home and at school for years to come.

8/2003 – Christopher began Physical Therapy (PT) to improve his strength, range or motion, gait, endurance, motor planning, balance, tactile defensiveness and safety awareness. He also began a home exercise program.

Christopher had impairments and functional limitations that affected his safe access to his school program that included: tightness in heel cords, decreased activity endurance, inefficient processing of vestibular and proprioceptive sensory input, weak postural control, impaired motor planning, inefficient bilateral motor coordination, decreased safety awareness and toe-walking.

12/2005 - Christopher participated in weekly Feeding Therapy, due to weight loss (1.8 pounds) and feeding challenges with sensitivity to smell and texture. He was found to be hyposensitive to taste. (To this day, he will "down" a bottle of hot sauce, if unattended.

Since Christopher's diagnosis of Autism in 2003, we seemed to live in clinics with treatment rooms resembling a childhood paradise. Mila was left by the wayside in the clinics watching Christopher seemingly have all the fun playing. And at home it was no different, because he had a team of ABA workers that occupied our home for all of his/their waking hours. How do you explain to a two-year-old that her brother zip-lining across the room, then dropping into a colorful ball pit was work not play? (You can't!)

Typical play dates were nonexistent. And, birthday parties... well, we were typically invited once until the parent(s) would witness Autism and some of the maladaptive behaviors associated with it from a bird's eye view. These behaviors made the other children and parents uncomfortable to the point that we were never invited again.

And, though we met lots of other children with Autism... well, their parents didn't necessarily want to have play dates either. Was your child low-functioning, have Asperger's Syndrome or was he somewhere in between? Was he impulsively violent or did he behave? My only hope of change for all of us, I believed, was to get Chris well by revolving our lives around therapies. But my daughter was too young to understand, and it led to jealousy, anger, resentment and sorrow.

I Love My Brother - Poem

"I HATE MY BROTHER," I heard her say
Why do we have to go to clinics every day?
All the attention, he always gets
And, off in a corner, alone I sit
I'm bored. I'm angry. I'm feeling down.
I wish my brother wasn't around
I want to have Autism too
If that's what it takes to spend more time
with you
I dropped to my knees and heaved a long
sigh
Lost control of my emotions and started to
cry
My baby girl, I love you so
One day, how much (I love you!) I hope
you'll know
I know you're going through a hard time
But what you said was out of line
Your brother fights every day
So that one day, words, he will be able to
say
And voice his opinions and make friends
and such
This explanation, to you, may seem a bit
much
"I'm sorry, Mommy, for what I said

Not sure what was going on in my head
I just want to have a brother who knows
how to play
I just want to have a brother who has words
to say
But if having a brother that talks all of the
time
Means I wont have the brother that now is
mine
I don't want another brother... mine is the
best!
Even though, sometimes, he can be quite a
pest...
"I LOVE MY BROTHER," I heard her say...

My Brothr Christeother
he is so cwte he like
bugs and spiters and he
scent of brds

It's Your Birthday! – 1/23/06

To my dearest Christopher,
Today you are six years old! I hope one
day you will know the depth of my love in
spite of all of my anticipated and
unexpected struggles. I wanted more than
anything else in life to be <u>your</u> mommy. I
love you and Mila to the depths of my
being. You two are my soul and the reason
my heart beats. I love you. Happy birthday!
(Happy face) My <u>eternal</u> love...

Love, Mommy! ~ 1/23/06
- From actual card

Therapies, Therapies...

2/2006 - A Functional Analysis Assessment was performed to develop a Behavior Support Plan.

3/2006 - A Behavior Intervention/ Behavioral Support Plan was put in place for behaviors that were impeding Christopher's learning. Christopher had delays with pragmatics.

4/2006 - An Assistive Technology Specialist said that Christopher would benefit from software-based language, which would allow for repetition or rehearsal with motivating audio-visual and animation features to sustain attention.

Our home was modified into an environment that would increase opportunities for sensory stimulation. In addition, I had it set up identical to his school environment for consistency across settings. Our life ='d therapies, therapies...

Easter - 2006

Dear Christopher,

I love you with all of my heart. I pray God will lead me on the correct path so that you will fully recover from autism, and be indistinguishable amongst your peers. I pray I can give you all that you need to survive in life. I made Mila just for you.

I worked so hard when you were a baby... Sometimes 20+-hour days, with the only breaks taken during your waking hours so we could bond. Then my body collapsed from pneumonia. I wanted another child so you could have a best friend and a playmate. I hope and pray that the two of you will always be close! I love you.

Love, Mommy!

- From actual card – Easter 2006

Therapies, Therapies... Therapies!

5/2006 – Christopher continued to have severe expressive and receptive language delays, secondary to a newly diagnosed developmental apraxia of speech.

6/2006 - OT Progress – Christopher had preferences for specific adults, and had difficulty functioning without them.

7/2006 – Chris began Biomedical Treatment with a Defeat Autism Now! (DAN!) Doctor. He started a Gluten-Free/Casein-Free Diet, B12 Shots, and supplements.

8/2006 - Christopher's test results showed that he was allergic to MOLDS and FOODS and was gluten intolerant.

I can always tell when Christopher eats gluten because his behavior changes almost immediately. He can't focus and becomes very silly and disorganized.

[He continues to be on a GF diet, and I have begun to remove all casein (again) in hopes of acquiring more positive change with his behavior.]

Food for Thought - Poem

With Autism, diet may be key
Some know it's true, while others don't see
Gluten-Free/Casein-Free (GFCF) may seem
quite a lot
If items are not easily store-bought
But some with Autism have a damaged gut
So certain dietary foods must be cut
The damage may have happened when the
child was born.
Some believe this theory... Others are torn
This damage comes from an immunological
injury
That's why with Autism diet may be key
Some ASD kids have an immune system
that's weak
Maybe the reason that some do not speak
Digestive problems can lead to a "leaky gut"
Which is why certain foods must be cut
Some food proteins pass through into the
bloodstream, only partially digested; it is so
These partially digested proteins have an
opiate-like affect; did you know?
They can bind to receptors, causing harmful
effects in the brain
Like a regular opiate, the affect is the same
An Opiates is a narcotics/drug; It is no ruse

So the proper types of food, you should always choose
"Autistic symptoms" no parent would want to magnify
Which is why the GFCF Diet, they try
With Autism, Diet may be key
Some know its true, while others don't see.

CHRIStmas – 2006

To my dear son, Christopher
I will never be able to explain or express my
love for you with mere words, though I pray
that you (one day) will be able to read and
understand my words to you. But if that
never happens, I plan to continue to show
you how much I love you and will love you
forever.

Love, Mommy! CHRIStmas 2006
- From actual card; drawing by Mila

Epileptic Seizures or Behavior Disorder?

1/2007 – A Neurological/Epilepsy Consultation revealed that Chris had paroxysmal episodes of aggressive behavior with spacing out, staring with right arm elevation. The EEG showed right front paroxysmal activity. (Depakote caused hysterical laughing.) Paroxysmal behaviors in patients with autism could be epileptic seizures or non-epileptic behavior disorder.

3/2007- There was a change in Chris's mental state. His behavior went from hyperactive to very subdued and passive. He began having tics. His eyes were constantly blinking and excessively bugged out. He pulled his own hair, though he was never previously self-injurious. He had major mood swings, episodes of zoning out, and was unresponsiveness to his environment.

4/2007 - Chris had episodes of various tics followed by aggressive/ combative and violent behavior. He screamed, cried, kicked, bit, and grabbed people. He was uncontrollable. His Neurologist thought he was in a postictal aggressive psychotic state. He had an MRI and EEG and was diagnosed with Complex Partial Seizure Disorder.

Dear Tooth Fairy

Dear Tooth Fairy,
Last night you did not give Christopher anything. I know you're not mean. Please give him something nice! Please give him something he really wants. Do you have kids? Do they go to school? Where do you live?

Love, Mila!
- From actual card

Dear Mom – 4/16/07

Dear Mom,
I love you mom. You're the best mom ever and you are very nice to me and you are cute all the time. I like when you buy toys for me and Christopher.

Love, Mila

Lights

5/2007 – Chris's medication increased and caused him to constantly/abnormally blinked fast, and he had frequent staring episodes. His Neurologist believed it was an absence status epilepticus. An EEG showed no evidence of this. He was believed to be on a Tegretol-induced absence status. Medication was discontinued. Christopher continued to have episodes of aggressive, combative behaviors.

7/2007 – Chris was diagnosed with dysarthria – a motor speech disorder that can occur as a developmental disability.

10/2007- Christopher began B12 shots (B12 shots seem to calm him vs. giving him energy, as is typical. (He has continued B12 shots.)

Christmastime 2007 - Initially, when Chris said a new word, I was so joyful that I gave him anything he desired. I stopped, realizing future problems may ensue, but never imagined it would have us surrounded by police cars/officers and flashing lights...

Lights - Poem

Loud music, bright lights
An extraordinary sight
Curling ribbon, pretty bows
Crowds of people, you know
White noise, enticing toys all within view
The hustle and bustle of Christmas is what
some do
The wrapping paper, he had to have
The wrapping paper, he tried to grab
But on this occasion, I firmly said, "No"
So I knew it was time to go (fast!)
A tantrum was coming, definitely
Too many times, it had happened to me
I glanced at the exit, making haste to the
door
For behaviors, no doubt, I knew were in
store
As I got to the exit, the wrapping paper, I
ditched
This is what triggered his incredulous fit
He kicked, hit, and started to shout
Customers were alarmed; I had to get out
Do you know how it feels when all eyes are
on you
When a child has a fit and there's nothing
you can do

Some judge you, and call you a bad mom
They assume it is you who is doing wrong
That parenting skills, for sure, you must lack
If a child of yours can so violently attack
Unfortunately, that's not the end of our day
He had a meltdown in the worst kind of way
He pulled my hair and repeatedly spat
Have you ever seen a child do that
I was parked in front, needing to make it to the door
None-the-wiser of what would occur exiting the store
He continued to kick, hit, and bite
His behavior/meltdown was a crazy sight
Most times when this happened, we were often ignored
But on this particular day, as we left the store...
People in cars witnessing this horrific sight
Called 911 regarding this struggle/fight
Two police cars came, four officers there stood
Didn't know how this situation could end up good
One knelt down beside me and asked me my name
Asked if I knew the reason why they came
I tried to answer their questions, being very polite
While my son continued his aggressive plight

At least a dozen calls, they did get
Said they saw a child and/or his mother
being hit
Some said it was me who was hitting my
child
Some said my child was acting scarily wild
Some said they had no idea what was going
on
But all said that something was very wrong
... A power struggle from a son who could
not speak
Who "tantrumed" over wrapping paper he
could not keep
I was trying to teach him that he could not
have everything he sought
I was trying to teach him that each item in
a store could/would not be bought
Sensory overload and Autism go hand-in-
hand
If you're familiar with special needs children,
you understand
The police officer's response: "What you're
saying is probably true, but we have a
different job to do, and we really need to
wrap it up."
The Officers got the paper just to see
I was concerned it would teach him it was
okay to "act out," to throw tantrums, kick
and hit

It would reinforce/encourage him to have future fits
They said they understood, but were put on the spot
So into the store, wrapping paper, they got
And, guess what... When they handed it to him, he immediately stopped
They looked surprised, then went on their way
"Sorry, ma'am," they said. "Have a nice day."
They shook their heads, smiled, and said, "You were right"
And inadvertently taught him the reward of a fight

Behavior Land

Autism was Christopher's first diagnosis, but not his last. Christopher was diagnosed with co-mormid conditions subsequently through the years that included but were not limited to: Severe expressive/receptive language disorder, sensory integration dysfunction, fine motor and gross motor delays. And, then there were the behaviors...

A behavior with a "typical" child can be bad. But a behavior with a child that is primarily non-verbal that uses his body to express his emotion takes "behavior" to a whole other definition. So, early on, Christopher (about age 3) had behaviors that included kicking, hitting, biting [you get the point, but the list goes on (and on).]

Some neurologists felt that the "behaviors" were undetected seizures. Other neurologists felt the contrary, that he was just having behavioral problems. Chris was diagnosed with seizures (First, complex partial seizures and eventually simple partial seizures) then, epilepsy. Other neurologists felt there was not enough evidence to diagnose him with seizures at all.

I refused putting Christopher on medication for "behaviors" associated with autism, because I felt/feel that medication only masks the underlying problem. I wanted to cure the problem. However, for seizures, I felt medicine was necessary. He had suspected seizures at age three, but it was not confirmed until 2007.

At age seven, Christopher began having tics, combined with what was diagnosed as "seizures with behavior manifestations." In less than a year, he was off of the medication, the seizures/tics stopped, and the behaviors lessened. If the seizures/tics were going to come back, though unpredictable, it was likely to come back when he hit puberty, I was told. Anyway, during the height of his suspected seizures, I took frequent unpleasant and unwanted journeys with him to what I'll call: Behavior Land.

Circus Freak Show

The seizures and/or "behaviors" were rampant. I learned how to safely restrain Christopher with proper hold techniques so that he would not hurt someone, himself or me. And Mila was so used to his "behavior(s)" that she became trained as well as Pavlov's dog with our protocol. In public, she quickly found a spot within eyesight of me, but far back enough to be out of the danger zone. Then, she would sit down until "it" was over.

("It" being Christopher screaming like he witnessed the dead come alive, and attacking me like I was a Lion (while countless people stared us down with looks of disgust, fear, pity or whatever emotion they felt with whatever they assessed our "situation" to be.) Mila would pretend to concentrate on her book, while I would concentrate on deescalating the "situation" with Chris like a fire extinguisher to a fire so we could evacuate. We withstood ridicule, pointing, gawking, and felt like unwilling participants in a circus freak show.

Autism and Aloneness - Poem

Autism (ASD) and Aloneness, you often see
But this occurrence doesn't have to be
Being apart from society is not necessarily
their choice
But dreams of inclusion is difficult to voice
Interaction may be a skill that they lack
They may get overwhelmed, when new
people they meet
One reason why they may tend to retreat
Imagine a life spent without anyone
Especially a child who is isolated from fun
Imagine it being just Y-O-U always/only
That kind of existence can be nothing short
of lonely
With not a single solitary friend around
Your voice limited to few or no sounds
Without equality, their behavior considered
unique
But isolation they do not intentionally seek
Envision the ASD population as being
socially deprived
Perhaps then, interaction you will strive (for)
Is it so hard to include someone who
cannot talk
Do you turn your back on someone if they
cannot walk

Here's what to expect:
Lack of eye contact or failure to respond
You may think they can't hear or something
is wrong
"Scripting" is when one repeats a phrase or
some words... (To you, it may seem
uncommon or absurd)
Perfect symmetry (perhaps) but in Autism,
few do exist
More commonly seen are behaviors that
persist, inappropriate behavior, and
resistance to change
They're ASD realities that you may label as
"strange"
Poor motor skills is another trait...
The child with ASD is often excluded from
"play dates"
"Typical" kids exhibit strange behaviors too
But with ASD it's the tenacity of their pursuit
When you meet someone with ASD, please
reach out
Include them even if they have nothing to
say
Include them when they don't look your way
Make the effort, and you will see
Autism and aloneness doesn't have to be
Togetherness...

Therapy is Key to Recovery

2/2008 – Chris saw a Doctor of Optometry (O.D.) for Vision Therapy to help with eye alignment, focus, movements, tracking/teaming, and visual processing. Christopher was identified to have trouble "crossing the midline." At school, I incorporated activities into his IEP that the O.D. recommended (tracking a figure 8 and a Marsden ball.)

3/2008 - Chris had success at school with Brain Gym activities to calm and organize him, the Handwriting Without Tears program, and the Alpha Smart for focus with spelling.

4/2008 – Chris began using a Bear Hug Weighted Wrap by Southpaw to help his significant difficulty with self-regulation, organization of behavior and sensory modulation... Music was very organizing for Chris's speech. The therapist discussed the use of music as a way to carry information so that he was able to receptively understand through music as well as (to) express his wants and needs by singing...

Therapy is key to recovery!

Happy Mother's Day!

Dear Mommy,
Happy Mother's Day, mommy! We love you and we hope you feel better soon. Christopher and I made a couple presents for you that we hope you like, which you probably will, because you always LOVE what we make you, which is AWESOME! It's your day and we celebrate you!!!

Love, Mila and Chris!
  • From actual card

Therapies & Introducing: Katherine McHugh

5/2008 – A Saturday program at Ability First in Pasadena gave Chris the chance to interact with peers and have fun!
Feeding Therapy continued to help with his hyper- and hyposensitivity to food texture, smell, etc. and to continue to improve his eating habits. OT was addressing Christopher's motor/sensory needs and reducing behavioral manifestations.
Behavioral Respite was implemented at a 1:2 ratio, due to aggressive behaviors.

5/2009 - Chris attended Say N' Play Speech Camp in Culver City; He was happy and had friends!

Summer 2009 – Christopher started Hyperbaric Oxygen Therapy (HBOT), and loved it! It was very calming for him and helped him focus, but was pricey.

9/2009 - Chris spent a year in public school in an Autism class but had electives and recess with typical peers.

4/2010 – ABA began with Katherine McHugh!

Thank You, Katherine McHugh - Poem

Thank you, Katherine McHugh
For everything each day you do
To teach my son, to help him grow
He loves you more than you may know
McHugh, Katherine is her name
Several months ago, to our home, she came
To help my son, she is a savior
She manages his maladaptive behaviors
She works with Christopher five days a week
Her goal: to get my son to speak
To teach him skills so he can play, and
behave in an appropriate way
This job is not for everyone; At times, it is
the antonym of fun
To see a child fall apart can break the
strongest heart
McHugh, Katherine, I want to say
Many therapists have come our way
But of your dedication, I will attest
You are amongst the very best

* It's sometimes hard to find a team of good,
dedicated persons in the special needs field; but
when you do, you feel like you've hit the jackpot.
Thank you, Katherine McHugh! And thanks to all
the other "Katherine McHugh's" in the world!!

(Above) Katherine, Mila, Christopher

Autism Doesn't Define Him!

4/2010 – Chris continues to have severe environmental and food allergies.

2/2011 – A three-day video EEG telemetry study revealed focal slowing seen over the frontocentral head region in both hemispheres that may indicate non-specific cerebral dysfunction.

5/2012 - Christopher began using a speech-generating device both in his educational setting and home to increase expressive language, improve auditory comprehension and pragmatic skills. Christopher has autism, but autism doesn't define him!

Autism Doesn't Define Him – Poem

He sees things a little differently
He has Autism, but that doesn't define him
Some people think he's kind of strange
While other "mean ones" call him names
They point, they laugh, and often stare
They act as though he's not right there
He repeats words; he stems/perseverates
He walks on his toes; He doesn't like to
wait
If you change his daily routine, he'll likely
act out
Sometimes he exhibits an unexplained shout
But if you look in his eyes, you'll see that
he's real
No hidden agenda, nothing to conceal
Doesn't know what it means to be shy
If you walk by him, he likes to say, "Hi"
(over and over)
He may get too close; he may give you a
hug
Some people get mad, while others just
shrug
He has a great big heart. Get to know him,
you'll see
His diagnosis is Autism, but Autism doesn't
define him

Love, Mila and Chris!

Dear Santa Claus,
Thank you very, very, very, very much for the card and all the presents that you have gotten for me and Chris. My mom is very happy that you got her the "Samantha Who" DVD's. Would you please try to get my mom a pink Vespa or something she might like. If you could get one for her, would you please wrap it up and pretend that it is from me so I could surprise her.

You can get me anything you feel like I should get. If you think I deserve a phone, would you try to get me one like Jillian's, but in gold? Thank you very, very, very, very, very much for everything. Oh, and would you try to get something Spiderman for Chris. Thank you. Merry Christmas to you, and Mrs. Santa Claus!

Love, Mila and Chris
- From actual card

Again

In 2010, Christopher began attending a non-profit school and therapy center in Buena Park, California. (He loves his teacher, aides and therapists!) He continues to have a severe receptive/expressive language disorder and articulation delays. He communicates by pointing or verbally in, mostly, single words with occasional longer phrases (3-4 words) when highly motivated. Though his verbal skills have increased, the intelligibility of his speech fluctuates and remains highly dependent on the context and familiarity of the listener.

Christopher is able to copy letters and words from chalkboard and paper, though his letter formation is not consistently legible. He is able to spell simple words and reads at a second grade level. He is able to add and subtract whole single digit numbers using Touch Math. He is able to recognize coins and dollars, and is learning basic time telling skills.

He is very affectionate (sometimes overly so.) He loves water fountains and the beach, but he continues to lack safety awareness. He loves taking pictures of things so that he can ask for help with spelling to "google" them. He is mesmerized by water and fire. Every year he asks Santa for a Duraflame Fireplace. (He wants to make S'mores and roast marshmallows.) He wants to travel the world to visit the M&M and Hershey's Chocolate stores worldwide.

5/2012 - Chris's behaviors had tapered off, and our atypical status quo became typical to us. He received a Student of the Year award in Occupational Therapy at school. We finally began to exhale. Then the seizures and tics that we saw at age seven came back full-force like a 9.5 earthquake. Puberty has arrived and changed our status quo once again. Devastatingly, he now meets all of the criteria to be diagnosed with Tourette's Syndrome. He was concurrently diagnosed with Mood Disorder – Not otherwise specified. We are in and out of the hospitals... again.

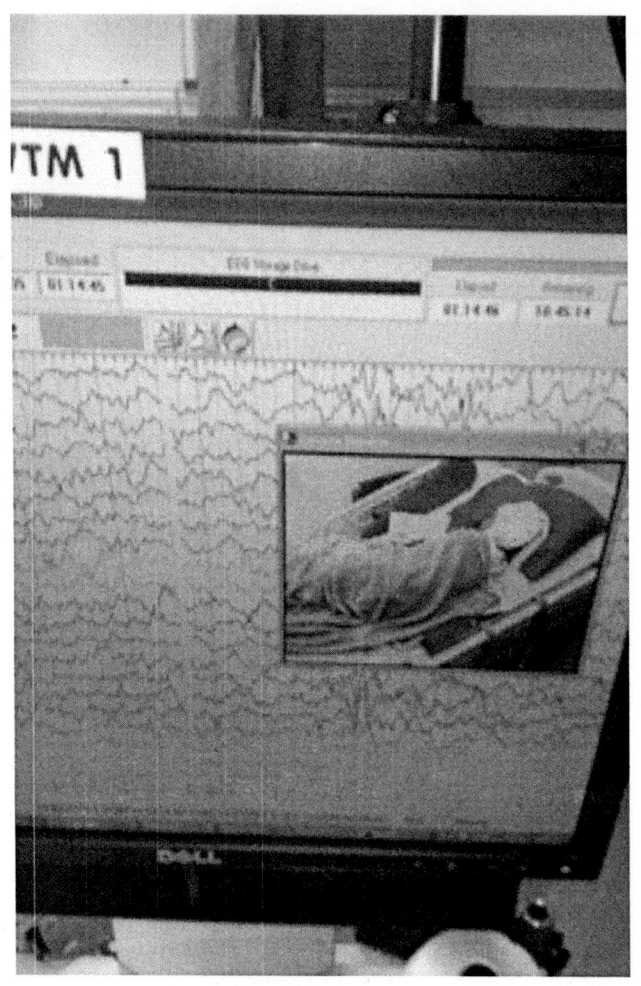

The Story of a Boy

Metaphorically: Gagged and bound
His voice makes limited sounds; His voice is
blind
Yet spoken thoughts converse in his mind -
Plots to unbind
Dreams of his speech and spoken words
Are these thoughts absurd
He bears witness to those who take for
granted their speech
His dreams of vocal expression out of reach
(for now)
He temporarily finds his voice in a SCREAM
Why does everyone frown, while he beams
They want to drown the voice he has found
They want to bring him DOWN, Down, down
If the tables were turned; and they, in turn,
yearned to find their voice...
Perhaps, they would see the beauty of a
scream
And/or attempt to discern what it may
mean
I believe the boy is finding his voice more
each day
Maybe tomorrow he'll have more to say

The End

Once upon a time there lived a "typical" atypical boy. Though there were other players of interest in this story; this was, in its simplest form, "The Story of a Boy" (and autism unawareness.) The end.

Epilogue

You'll Get Through This, You Will

Who caused my son's autism? Was it the nearly 19-hour labor before my inevitable C-section? What caused Chris's autism? Was it the immunization shot that put him in the hospital or the one after his MMR when he began to lose his speech? When/where did this happen? And, why? Did I do something wrong? Was it something in my environment? And, if not, how did this happen?

Will I be called a "Refrigerator Mom" or be accused of bad parenting, because my son's behavior is atypical. Was his autism psychological in origin or physiological in nature? How would I get through this without the answers to the 5 W's and One H? My best friend said, "You'll get through this. You will…"

You'll Get Through This. You Will - Poem

You'll get through this. You will
Why did this happen to my child
I had to ponder this a while
I feel guilt/shame. I feel like I'm to blame
I'm embarrassed; Sometimes, not
That I allowed those immunization shots
One friend said, "I gave my child
immunizations, like you. It could have
happened to my son too."
My friend, Dawn said: "It doesn't matter
who's to blame 'cause in the end, his
diagnosis wouldn't change"
My best friend, Enukshi, said: "You'll get
through this. You will."
That's when my tears began to spill
I cried (some for him) but also for me
I cried for the future I could no longer see
The future of his that I felt he was robbed
Is the reason for my inconsolable sobs
Will there be a day when my son and I will
talk
Will there be a day when we can go on an
unguarded walk
When I wont have to consciously hold his
hand
When the words that I speak, he
understands

I love my son; I want no other
Ecstatic that I am this boy's mother
I love to see his brilliant grin
Especially, knowing how tough his life's been
I just (sometimes) feel the need to mourn
The future I envisioned when he was born
If one day you feel like me
I hope you have the strength to see
You'll get through this, you will

Chris Will

I never forgot about my favorite "poster-saying" in college of the awesome mansion with multiple sports cars parked in front or of my "white picket fence theory." I have my 2.5 kids, but found that my knight in shining armor was me... aka "Bea." Now, don't get me wrong... a mansion with the fancy sports cars in front would be amazing, but my biggest dream in life is for Christopher to get well. Some think Christopher will never get better. Others aren't sure. As for me, I'm holding on to hope, because I will never let go of my biggest dream and mantra that one day "Chris Will."

Acknowledgements

With special thanks to my unofficial Editors: Mila Grace, Henrietta Johnson and Dawn Buchanan.

And to my grandmothers: Helen Grace Johnson and Beatriz Mendoza Ramirez With my eternal love... And, as promised!!

ABC School, Duarte
Ability First, Pasadena
Applied Behavior Consultants, Inc.
Assistive Technology Exchange Center
Autism Research Institute/Bernard Rimland –
(Letter in Support of ABA)
Behavior Functions, Inc. (Katherine McHugh)
Behavioral Intervention and Training Team
(Carla Walden)
California Integrative Hyperbaric Center
Casa Colina Children's Services
Center for Developing Kids
Children's Hospital, Los Angeles
CHOC Children's – Children's Hospital of
Orange County
CHOC Pediatric Subspecialty Faculty
Eastbluff Elementary School
Descanso Pediatrics (Jean Chou, M.D.)
Eastern Los Angeles Regional Center
Elliot Institute (Rosie Quezada, M.A.)
Frank D. Lanterman Regional Center (Enrique
Roman, Service Coordinator)
Focus
Gallagher Pediatric Therapy
Glendale Adventist Medical Center – Pediatric
Therapy Center (Lauren N. Penoliar, OTR/L)
Harper Clinic/ABA
Hear Center
Hjelte-Phillips Speech and Language Center
HOAG Memorial Hospital

Holding Hands (Juan/Floor Time, Lori/Dance & Movement Therapy)
Huntington Memorial Hospital
Karen H. Chao, O.D. (Developmental Optometrist)
Karima Hirani, MD MPH
Los Angeles Speech & Language Therapy Center, Inc. (Say N' Play Speech Camp)
Lovaas Institute for Early Intervention
Mandana Moradi, Psy.D.
Mission Hospital
Newport Integrative Health, Koren Barrett, ND
Pasadena Child Development Associates
Providence Speech and Hearing Center
Regional Center of Orange County (Denise Zerra, Service Coordinator)
Rose Bowl Aquatic Center
Scottish Rite of Orange County
Speech and Language Development Center (Lisa McGuire... and all of Christopher's teachers, therapists and aides & Harriet H.)
Spirit League
The Children's Therapy Center
The Epilepsy and Brain Mapping Program
UCI Medical Center Neurodevelopment & Behavioral Clinic (Gail E. Fernandez, M.D., Anne Tournay, MRCP(UK), Christy Hom, Ph.D.)
UCLA Healthcare
UCLA Medical Center

UCLA Neuropsychiatric Hospital (Sarah Spence, M.D.)
UCLA's Autism Evaluation Clinic (B.J. Freeman, Ph.D., Beverly K. Johnson, Psy.D., Pegeen Cronin, Ph.D.)
Villa Esperanza Services (all of Christopher's teachers and aides and Casey G.

(More to come!)

About the Author

Beatriz Fox graduated from Loyola Marymount University with a degree in Screenwriting and has been a member of SAG/AFTRA since 1993. She is an advocate for autism awareness and has been active in the autism community since 2003. Beatriz lives with her family in Newport Beach.

http://meant2bea.blogspot.com/

http://chriswillblog.wordpress.com/

http://facebook.com/meant2bea/

https://twitter.com/_meant2bea/